# ZAC POWER™
## TEST DRIVE

# ZAC'S ICY POLE

BY H. I. LARRY

ILLUSTRATIONS BY ANDY HOOK, RON MONNIER & ASH OSWALD



hardie grant EGMONT

# CHAPTER... ...ONE

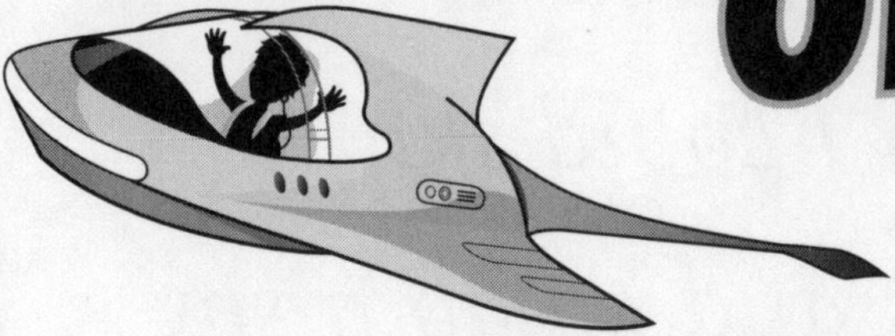

On the first day of school, it was hot. Zac Power wished he was outside. He wanted to go for a swim.

He felt like eating an ice-cream.

*I wish I could skip maths and go on a spy mission right now,* he thought.

Zac Power was 12 years old. He was a spy for a group called GIB.

TOP SECRET

But no-one at school knew that. It was top secret! His brother Leon and his mum and dad were all spies for GIB, too.

All GIB spies had code names.
Zac's code name was Agent Rock Star.
Leon's code name was Agent Tech Head.

Leon made gadgets for GIB and Zac got to test drive them.

Zac loved being a spy. He got to test drive fast cars and all the cool spy gadgets. Zac also went on the best missions ever!

# CHAPTER... ...TWO

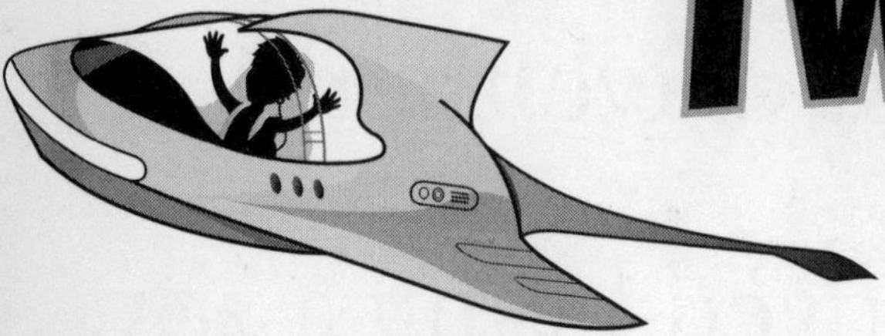

At last, the bell for the end of school went.

Zac ran out the door.

He walked up the hill to his house.

At the top of the hill
was an ice-cream van.
*Yum!* thought Zac.
*Just what I need*.

He bought a rocky
road ice-cream.
It was his
favourite
kind.

The ice-cream had little chocolate rocks and roads running across it!

He took a big bite. The ice-cream was nice and cold. Then he bit into something hard.

'Ouch!' he said as he hurt his tooth.

But then he realised what it was.

*It's a GIB disk!* Zac thought. He looked to see if anyone was watching. But there was no-one around.

Zac got out his SpyPad. The SpyPad was a phone and a laser. It could crack codes. And it had cool games!

Zac put the disk into his SpyPad. A message flashed on the screen.

Zac smiled. 'Awesome! GIB needs me.'

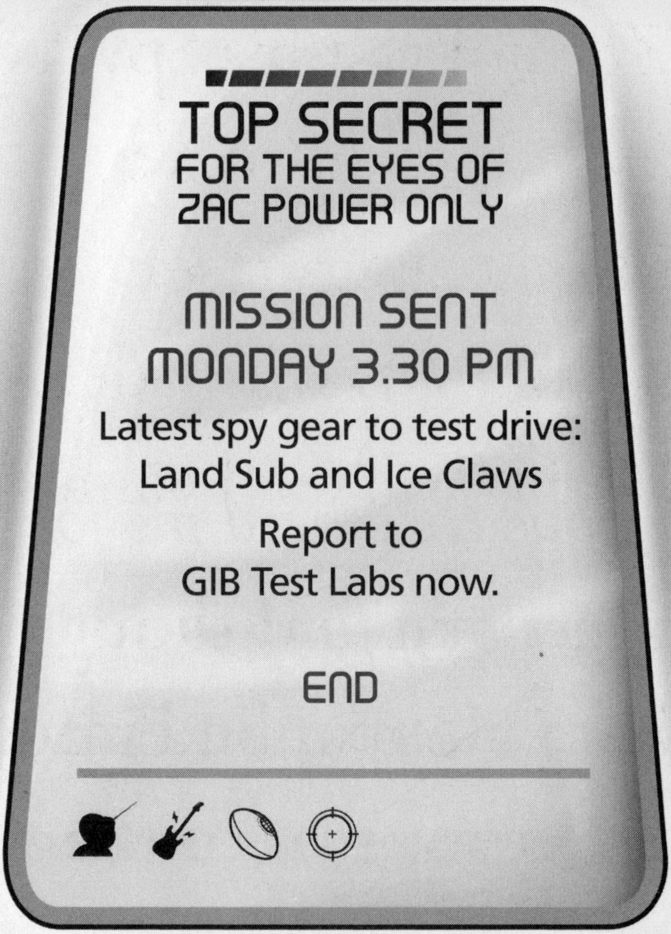
TOP SECRET
FOR THE EYES OF
ZAC POWER ONLY
MISSION SENT
MONDAY 3.30 PM
Latest spy gear to test drive:
Land Sub and Ice Claws
Report to
GIB Test Labs now.
END

The screen changed.

*I hope they need me for something fun!* thought Zac. He climbed into the front seat of the ice-cream van.

'Hello, Agent Rock Star,'

said the ice-cream man. 'I'm Agent Snow Cone. Put your seatbelt on. I'll be driving you to the GIB Test Labs.'

'Cool!' said Zac. The van drove off to the beach.

# CHAPTER... ...THREE

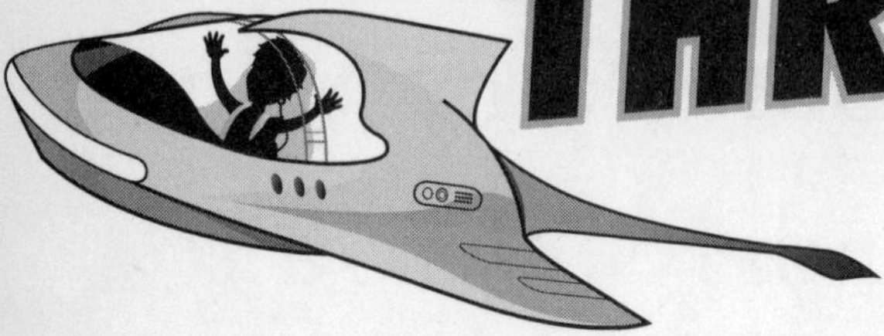

The van stopped.
Zac climbed out.
He was in the GIB Test Labs. There were cool gadgets everywhere.

Zac could see rockets and lasers and space suits. Zac's brother Leon was waiting.

'We've got some cool stuff for you to test drive, Zac,' said Leon.

'You'll be testing ice claws and a sub.'

'Awesome!' said Zac.

'The land sub is the best we've ever had,' said Leon. 'It is super fast and goes on land as well as in the water. It's waiting for you outside.'

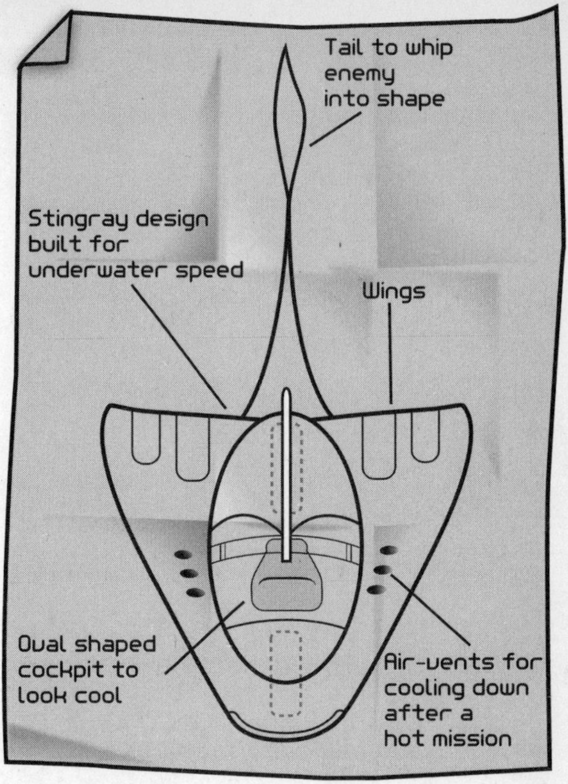


Zac picked up the ice claws. 'What do these do?' he asked.

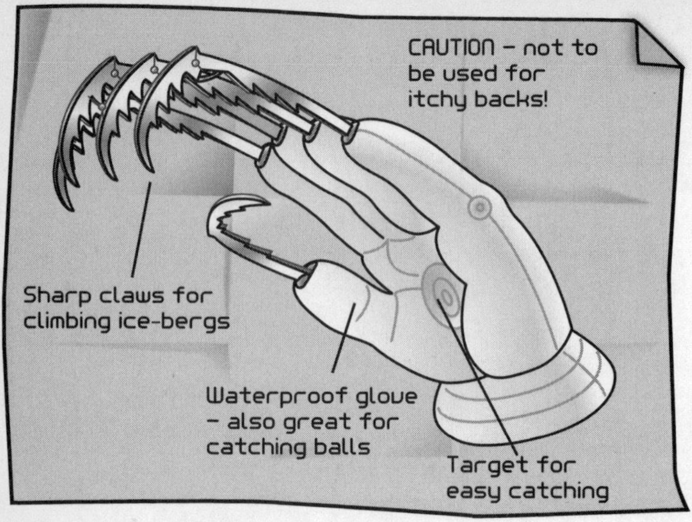


'They help you to climb in icy places,' said Leon. 'Push the buttons.'

Zac hit a button. Metal claws popped out.

Suddenly Zac's SpyPad went off.

**BEEP-BEEP-BEEP**

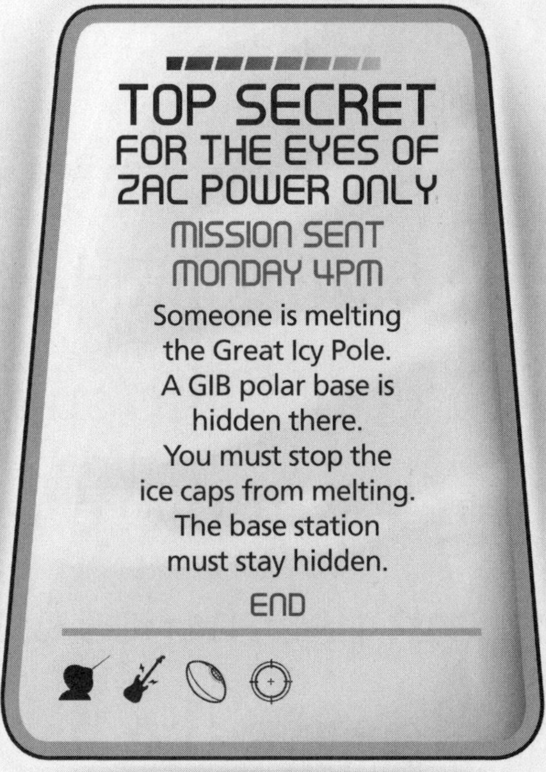
TOP SECRET
FOR THE EYES OF
ZAC POWER ONLY
MISSION SENT
MONDAY 4PM
Someone is melting
the Great Icy Pole.
A GIB polar base is
hidden there.
You must stop the
ice caps from melting.
The base station
must stay hidden.
END

'GIB needs me for a mission!' said Zac. 'Someone is melting the ice caps!'

'That's where the GIB polar base is hidden,' said Leon. 'The sub will get you there. You can use the ice claws to help save the base.'

Zac grabbed the ice claws. 'How do I get to the sub?' he asked.

'This way. **HURRY!**' said Leon.

# CHAPTER... ...FOUR

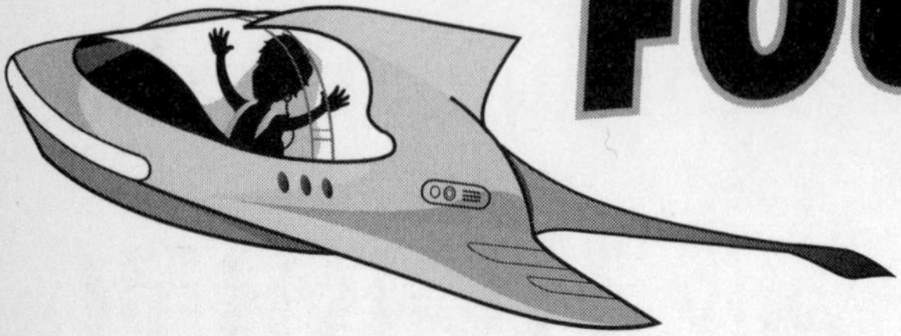

Leon pressed a green button on the wall. The wall in front of Zac opened like a door. He saw a big pipe like a giant water slide. Water was running down it.

'The sub is waiting for you at the bottom of the pipe,' said Leon. He gave Zac a wetsuit and a box with a red button on it.

Zac put on the wetsuit.

He jumped into the pipe. Zac sped down the pipe. He went around bends. He **SPLASHED** through lots of water.

*This is way better than a water slide*, Zac thought.

Suddenly, Zac flew out of the pipe and

landed in the sea.
He swam around, but he couldn't see a sub.
*The sub must be hidden,* Zac thought. *Where is it?*

He looked at the box Leon had given him. The red button had something written on it:

Zac pushed the button. He could hear a

WHOOSHING

noise. Then the sea started to bubble.

*Sweet*, thought Zac. *The sub is coming*.

Then Leon's face popped up on Zac's

SpyPad. 'Don't forget to file your test drive report,' said Leon.

Zac sighed. He loved doing test drives, but he hated writing reports.

Suddenly the sub came up. It was the coolest sub Zac had ever seen! There were rockets on its back. It had two wings. There were two big wheels under it.

Zac got in and sat in the seat. He pushed

a button on the dashboard. He heard a noise. But the sub didn't start.

Instead, a big TV screen popped up. It was huge.

There was also a big popcorn maker. *That will be good for the trip,* Zac thought.

Then Zac found the sub's start button and pushed it. The sub went down to the bottom of the sea. Then it took off at high speed.

Zac was off to the ice caps!

*Time for a movie and popcorn*! Zac thought, and he turned the popcorn maker on.

5 flavours to choose from:
Honeybee, Choc Supreme,
Sea salt, Crunchy Crazy
and Pop Hearts
Hover lid design
for extra poppy
pop corns!
Side fins
to make
popcorn
go faster
Heavy duty
metal case
for mega popping!
Big round
ON button
for quick
starting
CORN EASY

The movie had only just started when the screen flashed.

YOU ARE
AT THE
ICE CAPS

*Already?* Zac thought. *Leon was right. This sub is super fast!*

# CHAPTER... ...FIVE

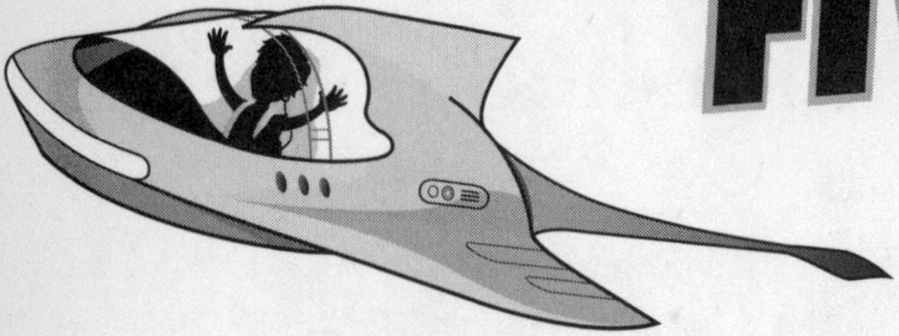

The sub hit something with a **BANG** and stopped. Zac looked up. There was a great icy mountain in front of him.

*Wow! It's the Great Icy Pole*, thought Zac. He could see the top. But it was a long way up. *It's lucky this sub can go on land, too,* Zac thought.

Zac started the sub again. It moved quickly over the snow.

Suddenly . . .

Something was hitting the sub. Huge snowballs were coming from the ice caps! There was lots of melting snow.

Zac couldn't see where he was going. The ice caps were melting fast. Snow was coming down on top of him!

*I've got to get out of here!* Zac thought.

He turned the sub's wipers to turbo top-speed.

The wipers went up. They looked like hands. They started catching the snowballs.

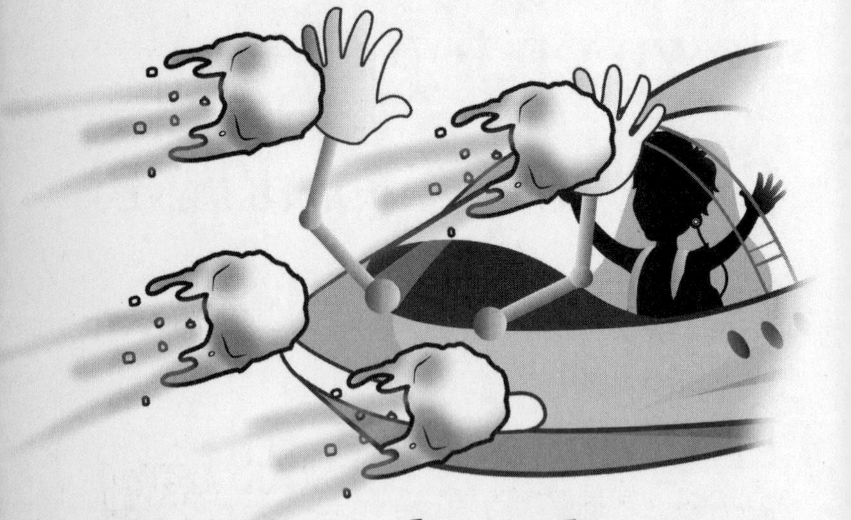

*Awesome*, thought Zac. *Now I can go even faster.*

He reached the side of the Great Icy Pole and looked up.

He saw a black box at the very top of the Great Icy Pole. It had two words written on it:

Then, he saw a chopper.
A pink chopper!

*That chopper belongs to the BIG twins, Pinkie and Britney,* thought Zac.
*I knew BIG was behind this!*

BIG was an evil spy group. They were GIB's biggest enemy. They must have turned the heating unit on!

Zac turned the sub off. He had to climb up to the heating unit. Zac put the ice claws on.

He hit the button and the claws came out. He started to climb.

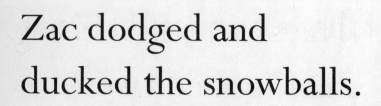

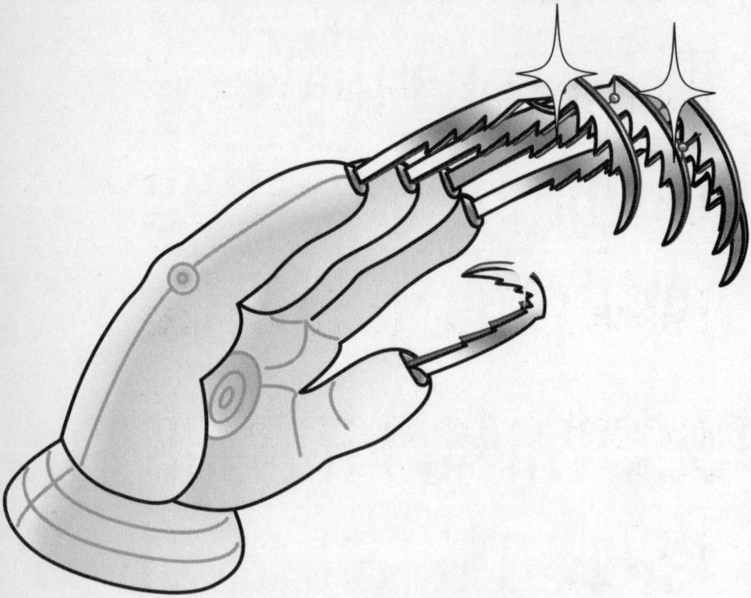

Zac dodged and ducked the snowballs.

If a snowball hit him he would fall into the sea. But he kept climbing. He was close to the heating unit now. Zac knew he needed to turn it off – but how?

The snow was melting. Zac climbed faster.

He could already see some of the GIB polar base. There was no time to lose!

He reached the heating unit. There were cords coming out of it.

Zac cut the cords with his ice claws.

Zac looked around for the evil twins. Then he heard a noise above him. The twins were in their pink chopper.

They were getting away!

They were writing a message in the sky.

But Zac knew better. The polar base wouldn't be there when the twins came back.

GIB moved it every two weeks to keep it top secret!

# CHAPTER... ...SIX

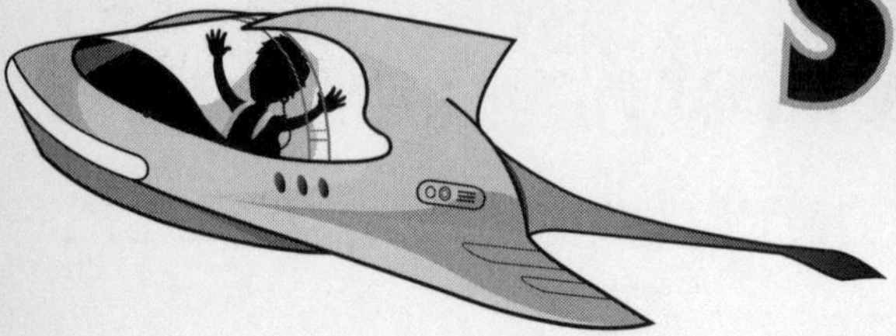

Zac took off the ice claws. His hands were cold. He pulled out his SpyPad and sent a message to GIB.

The polar base
is safe.
BIG agents
got away.

An answer came back from Leon:

Key in the number 9227.
Enter polar base.
Then return to
GIB Test Labs.

Zac typed in the numbers on the wall of the polar base.

A secret door opened. Zac walked into the polar base.

There was a sled inside. Zac jumped on. He slid all the way down the Great Icy Pole to his sub.

Zac climbed into the sub. He put his iPod

on and turned his favourite song up loud.

Zac looked at his SpyPad again. There was a new button on his screen.

Zac clicked the Test Drive button. He groaned. He had almost forgotten about the test drive report! He sighed and started writing the report.

Just as he finished his report, he arrived back at the lab.

Leon was waiting for him.

'Well done, Zac!' said Leon.

'Thanks,' said Zac.

He saw Agent Snow Cone standing next to the ice-cream van.

'I'm glad you're still

here,' said Zac. 'I need another ice-cream!'

'You've done well,' said Agent Snow Cone. 'Have a free one.'

'I need your test drive report, Zac,' reminded Leon.

'All done!' said Zac.

Then he helped himself to a huge ice-cream.

# TEST DRIVE
## REPORT

## SUBMERSIBLE LAND SUB

Rating:

The sub was super fast. It was so fast I didn't even get to watch my movie or eat my popcorn! I felt ripped off.

## ICE-CLAWS

Rating:

These were great for extreme climbing. I couldn't have climbed to the top of the ice cap without them. They are cool.

END

# ...THE END...